The Creeping Charlies

By Rebecca Maye Holiday

Copyright © Rebecca Maye Holiday 2022

The Creeping Charlies / Rebecca Maye Holiday

Fiction – Horror

ISBN: 978-1-7776821-4-9

No part of this book may be reproduced, stored in or introduced into a retrieval system, or transmitted in any form or by any means (electronic, mechanical, photocopying, torrent, recording or otherwise), without the prior written permission of the author, unless quoting small portions of text for critical reviewing, reporting or educational purposes.

Interior text and author photo © Rebecca Maye Holiday, 2022.

Written in the province of Nova Scotia, Canada.

The Creeping Charlies

The Creeping Charlies

y name?

It's Collette Charlie, but my friends and my brother call me Collie. I'm fourteen years old.

I like sitting in the window seat of my dusty old bedroom, writing in the ruled blue lines of my notebook. I like to dream. I used to dream of having a story to write down, to share with other people... now I only dream of breaking free from my life's story altogether.

There are four of us in my family: there's Mamma, Papa, my older brother Pierre, and then me, the youngest. Sometimes, being the youngest sibling is a blessing. Less responsibility, less expected of me... and other times, being the youngest is a curse. It means more time to myself, more time gazing out at the leaf-strewn streets and milky white skies of this dusty little neighbourhood.

I can sometimes remember the blue skies, back when living in Charogne Falls still felt like swimming through one vivid, perfect summer day. That was a long time ago. The skies now are thick and sultry with a haze of rancid humidity, and it never lifts, except for in the winter months... and even then, the sky is never blue. It's a pale gray, dry and barren and as stark as our futures here.

The Creeping Charlies

We live in a large gray house, Edwardian style, three storeys tall if you care to count the attic. It has a huge front porch with an overhead roof supported by many tall white columns, a skeleton swept over with dust and dead vines. It's my chore to keep the porch free of the dead leaves constantly thrashing against everything in the bitter wind, so I keep an old corn broom just inside the front entryway closet for such daily occasions. It would be nice, I sometimes think, if somebody would stop by and have a conversation with me, but conversations are few and far between here.

I always keep an eye out for Pierre coming down the street, haggard and gaunt and exhausted, because by then, I know it's five o' clock. Pierre returns home at the same time every afternoon. He's paid well for his work, but all things considered, it will still never be enough. Like most younger men in Charogne Falls, Pierre's been tasked with spraying down the structure of the Charogne Pesticides Factory, which is done in shifts twenty-four hours a day, using thick hoses and leaden water to dampen down the vapours. It's not a thankless job, but I'm glad I don't have to do it.

✠✠✠

Mamma and Papa have taken to calling them zombies, but that's not really what they are.

For one thing, no zombie is coherent or clever enough to so deceptively manage to retain the soul of a loved one, not just physically, but also in terms of personality. In most ways, they're the very same people they always used to be.

Take the mayor, for example. Mayor Seymour Black is a handsome man with chestnut-brown hair and an ever-pleasant smile, or at least, he used to be. One time, when I was in Grade Four, he visited my classroom during a writing contest. *"You keep on filling those old notebooks, writing down those thoughts, young lady,"* he'd advised after reading one of my stories, *"and when you're rich and famous, I'll be first in-line to get my autographed copy."*

Mayor Black spends most of his time now skulking and pacing through the town cemetery under the sweeping shadows of the beech trees that litter the area. His skin, pasty and pale and green, hangs loosely on his face. Dark bags linger beneath jaundiced eyes, and his suit, which he hasn't changed in years, is worn and filthy with mold. By day, he's harmless, just another lost soul among many in a dying town.

It's at night when we have to worry. I've never once forgotten to deadbolt the front and back doors to the house, and one evening, about two years ago, Papa came home with a great big bag of cement slung over his burly shoulders, whistling a cheerful tune as he trudged into the house.

"What's that for?" I'd asked, crouched on the staircase landing.

"We need to fill in the root cellar," huffed Papa. *"Door's made of wood, so the latch won't be strong enough to hold back anything... there's some plywood up in the attic, and I want you and Pierre to grab a hammer and start boarding up the windows on the bottom floor."*

I understood completely by then.

See, we had a cat once, Cucumber, our family pet. Not a purebred cat or anything, just some sort of tabby mix, but we loved him all the same. It was early in the morning, when

The Creeping Charlies

the sky was still dark as death itself, that we woke up to see two of the liquidators who Pierre worked with, Blaise and Claude, cornering Cucumber in the driveway, grappling for the poor cat's legs as he struggled to hide under the car. Papa tried to hit both men with a hockey stick, but they just dragged Cucumber away screaming in shrill desperation... and we haven't seen him since.

It was chilling. They were all over him. There was nothing left. They actually backed away with what was left of him in their mouths.

Mamma just stood there on the front porch and burst into tears, sinking to her knees. Cucumber had been her best friend, her little kitchen partner who sat on the countertop and watched her while she cooked, her comfort during those depressing afternoon talk shows on the TV. It seems more and more lately that friends are difficult to come by in Charogne Falls.

Anyway, they've never attacked a person, at least, not that any of us know of. I don't consider them zombies at all, and if a simpler reason for that is needed, then it's because zombies in the movies always accept what they are and hunt on instinct, like vicious dogs. The people living here with us in the shaded forests and gloomy cul de sacs of Charogne Falls are by no means that. I know they felt terrible, because the very next day after Cucumber was taken, a basket of chocolates and fresh fruit was left on the doorstep, addressed to our family. There was no excuse written on the note included, no rambling promises that it wouldn't happen again, nothing like that.

The Creeping Charlies

The note in the basket only had four small words written there, or rather, scribbled there: *please understand... please forgive.*

It frightens me horribly that my brother's a liquidator, because the liquidators put themselves at such a great risk! The liquidators are always the ones most likely to decay and twist apart, even if only gradually, and it can't be noticed at first. It begins harmlessly enough... they might start forgetting the smallest things, like the first movie they ever watched, or their license plate number. Then, invariably I think, the pacing begins, and the irritability. They start snapping at people over the silly petty things and fixations on death and dying swoop over them like a shroud. I've seen them poking at roadkill with a stick, or sometimes going out with hunting rifles into the forest for days at a time, returning covered in sweat and blood. *"Sorry,"* they always tell their families, *"we didn't mean to be so late getting back."* Their sour breath and jittery fingers overwhelm them, and before you know it...

Well, not Pierre. Pierre is too careful for that. He never scoffs at the safety protocols, never smirks at the warning signs, never sets foot on the premises of Charogne Falls Pesticides itself. I don't know why he'd *want* to, anyway. The factory made mostly pesticides and agricultural poisons, and whatever caused the accident, whatever caused... *this*... isn't something I've ever dared to ask about. I've heard the rumours, the hushed whispers, and I try not to let those things occupy my imagination.

The Creeping Charlies

It doesn't matter anymore. What matters is that I've got an exit plan.

✠✠✠

"Well, well, well!" Pierre exclaims in a rush of breath as he pulls off his mask and goggles, setting them aside on the porch. "If it isn't my kid sister, killing time as usual."

That's a joke between us. Better to be killing time, after all, than to be killing *other* things.

Despite the humidity that clouds the air around us, it's cold outside. I bring my hands down into the sleeves of my brown pullover sweater and bite my lip, waiting for the frigid temperature to pass. Autumn is coming. I can smell it in the air, because the flaming bonfires that fill the backyards of Charogne Falls are one of the few things that can counter the vast nothingness otherwise permeating the town. As the nights grow longer and the rooftop shingles curl up hideously in the frost, bonfires become a sacred ritual for most of us, a space where we can gather in the warmth and feel safe.

Pierre runs a nervous hand through his thick black hair and gazes up at the sky.

"What is it?" I ask, staring.

Pierre smiles, but it's strangely not a very happy smile. "I was talking with Mamma and Papa last night, Collie. In just another few days or so, we'll have enough money to move out of Charogne Falls altogether."

"Really?" I can barely contain my excitement, and my voice comes out as a sort of crooked squeal.

"Shhh, quiet down, Collie! I wasn't supposed to tell you yet. Besides, if the neighbours overhear, you know it'll just make them feel more hopeless, and that'd be a rotten thing right now, what with the autumn season coming up."

Pierre's right, I guess. Most of the other townsfolk of Charogne Falls moved out years ago, packing up quickly with the help of hired moving companies and fleeing in the night, out to other towns and cities elsewhere in Canada, probably. Those of us who stayed here had no choice. We were the ones with the bills we couldn't afford to pay, the student loan debt we couldn't afford to carry in another place, the houses we couldn't afford to give up, and so, begrudgingly, we lingered on with our small grants from the federal government, and maybe the occasional drive into the next town for groceries now and then. We can only blame ourselves for choosing to stay. We weren't *forced* to live here. We could have packed up and left whenever we wanted to.

Life doesn't always work that way, though.

There's a sharp snap, the unmistakable sound of twigs breaking, of leaves crunching underfoot, and Pierre leaps in front of me, pushing me towards the door. "Get in the house, Collie," he orders, "*now*."

"Why? Just because you're older than me, doesn't mean you get to boss me around, Pierre..."

"Just go!" Pierre insists, and the savageness of his voice is like the cold steel slice of a knife against my skin. It's enough to get me to yank open the rusty screen door and dart behind it, anyway. In the sleeves of my pullover, my hands are trembling. As the wind picks up, I wonder whether to go find Mamma and Papa or call for help.

𝒯he 𝒞reeping 𝒞harlies

The dead brown needles of the yew shrub in the street's garden patch shake and shudder, and I have to clap my hands over my mouth to keep from gasping out loud when I realize it's not the wind making it happen... something's in there. Something alive.

Or maybe *not* something alive, and that's the most dreadful thought of all.

"Collie, didn't you hear what I said?" Pierre hisses under his breath. "Get in the house and bolt the door shut behind you!"

I can't move, and not because I don't want to listen. I'm frozen to the spot, and when I try to step back closer towards the house, I find myself stumbling over my own two feet.

"Go!" Pierre insists again, waving his hand back...

And then a small tawny fawn trots out from behind the shrub, and pauses to stare at us both. Its great big black eyes are wide with fear, its little nose quivering as it sniffs the air. The wind ruffles the soft white speckles in its fur like gentle fingers brushing by.

I finally gather the courage back to step out from behind the screen door, sighing in relief. "Just a stupid deer," I laugh with a shudder. "You worry too much, Pierre."

Pierre hasn't moved just yet. He's gripping the white wooden columns that support the shingled awning of the porch, his eyes shining.

"Let's go in," I urge. "Mamma's making smoked meat sandwiches for supper."

"Smoked meat," Pierre mumbles as he watches the fawn amble away. "...Sounds great."

The Creeping Charlies

I notice, as we both make our way into the house, that Pierre is licking his lips, glancing back over his shoulder. It doesn't bother me, though. We'll be leaving Charogne Falls soon, and with it, everything bad and ugly in the air that gets its hold on people.

✠✠✠

Nights are awkward in Charogne Falls.

For one thing, we block all the windows on the upper floors at night, using heavy antique furniture. Mamma always helps me to shove my old oak wardrobe from Grandma Rhoda up against my bedroom window, and it doesn't get slid back into place until the light of the day is long underway. We've already put a padlock on the attic door, nailing it shut, and whenever a brand-new hole appears torn in the walls anywhere, Papa promptly boards it up with scrap wood, or whatever other supplies we've got lying around.

"There!" Mamma says with a gasp of breath, leaning herself against the tall wardrobe and pushing it up against the side of the window seat, blocking it completely. "That should do it."

I tug at the sleeve of my pajama top, just a force of habit, and before I know it, the words just slip out. "Are we ever going to leave Charogne Falls, Mamma?"

Mamma flashes me one of those stern, tired looks of hers, her dark eyes weary, her long blonde hair a mess because she no longer bothers to style it anymore. "Please don't ask me things like that, Collette."

"It's just... I... I'm *scared*, Mamma."

"I know."

The Creeping Charlies

"I'm scared for Pierre."

"So am I."

Mamma and I used to have long, goofy conversations with each other over clothes and makeup and boys, and I miss that. Nowadays, our conversations are reduced to choppy exchanges here and there, unspoken truths lingering but never said aloud.

I know that Mamma's lonely. She used to play weekly bingo, or be baking little peanut butter squares with rainbow marshmallows in them for the neighbourhood potlucks. She used to be in a book club at the public library. Since the accident, her paperback copy of *The Bell Jar* has just sat there on the arm of the sofa, dog-eared and completely untouched since that very day so long ago. I've thought of moving it numerous times. Whenever it's my turn to dust and clean the parlour, I always reach out to pick up the book and put it up on the shelf... but I never really do. I work around it, and no matter how much I'm scolded for it, nobody else in the family ever picks up that book to put away, either.

It's a lot easier to accept the future, which has endless potential, than to accept the past, which none of us chose and which none of us can really change. Mamma thinks so, at least. "It's no good," she tells me, sitting on the edge of my bedroom mattress, "dwelling on what upsets us. We're all in this together, Collette."

I loathe that phrase. *We're all in this together*, people repeat like a stale mantra over and over again, but some of us are in it a lot deeper than others.

The Creeping Charlies

"Try to get some rest," Mamma encourages, "or read a book or something if you can't sleep."

"I will, Mamma."

"And, Collette... remember to leave your bedroom light on."

"Alright... goodnight, Mamma."

"Goodnight."

Mamma's right. I won't be able to sleep at all.

At least I've got my library books. Ms. Richings, the town librarian, used to be at the helm of the Charogne Public Library... well, she still *is*, but in a different way. Books are no longer checked out. Ms. Richings is far too busy burrowing her way between the drywall and the brick of the library building, hunting for rats and mice to feed on, stirring up asbestos fibres. She keeps a yellow notepad and a pen on the front desk. "Just write down the title of whatever book you take," she snapped at me the last time I spoke to her, hunched down on the floor, chewing on her own fingernails. "Books don't matter. Words and pictures don't matter." She picked away at her own face, fingers skittering, thin sheets of wet yellow skin sloughing from her cheeks. "Go home, little girl."

My library books were overdue by a few weeks. I had a small stack, mostly just well-worn Apple paperbacks and a couple of movie novelizations, and I'd read them all, with no new books coming to me in what felt like ages.

I'll buy myself some new books when we leave Charogne Falls.

As usual, my night is a restless one. Just when I've drifted off to sleep, warm and relaxed beneath my soft cotton

The Creeping Charlies

quilt, noises jolt me awake again, sounds of scrabbling and scraping and horrid, ugly moaning.

They're on the lawn, dozens of them. Their eyes are like seeping wounds, rimmed red with a crust of dry pus at the corners, and their clothes are ragged and unwashed. Their fingernails are soiled with dried blood, their faces a rancidly creamy green, and their skin has bubbled up and lifted in various patches. I cover my ears with my pillow and groan, frustrated. Why do they have to be so annoying? Why can't they just go away?

They're sick, I try to remind myself as I hear one of them let out the most peculiar curdled wheezing noise. *They're sick, and they don't mean anything by it.*

Poor things.

✠ ✠ ✠

Mamma watches me like a hawk from the parlour window whenever Sasha La Fleur stops by for a visit.

Sasha and I are best friends. We met on our first day of kindergarten, and we've always been inseparable. We told ghost stories in the forest after school, climbing high up in the trees with our high-top platform shoes carefully balanced on the branches so we could stand and shout silly jokes to one another. We'd begged Papa to build us a treehouse there, so we'd have a better place to play. *"I'll get around to it someday, girls,"* he always promised, but then Sasha's mother was working in the factory when the accident happened, and that very same night, Sasha's mother staggered helplessly through the dark and back to her house, and Sasha's mother died in there.

The Creeping Charlies

I don't know exactly how it all went down for Sasha that night, or for Sasha's father, whose face has long-since gone cloudy and lifeless with grief, but I never ask. All I know is what I've heard Mamma and Papa whispering to each other after they think Pierre and I have fallen asleep...

"Her skull was fractured, split like a broken dish, and half her brain was just... wasn't..."

"At least she's dead now. It's disgusting of me to say, I know, but at least she's not suffering anymore."

Sasha and I like to sit on the front porch together and bounce a rubber ball with a pretty green-and-purple marble pattern on it back and forth. The ball was in the back of my bedroom closet for the longest time, in the little nook where I've stuffed all my teddy bears and picture books and childish things away, never really able to bear the sheer thought of disposing of them. I like to chat idly while I bounce the ball. Sasha, her eyes a pale silvery-gray, her once glossy golden hair now knotted and matted with dried blood, mostly just listens to me.

"We should have another sleepover sometime soon," I tell her, which of course is a flat-out lie, all things considered, but I'm too tired of it all to care anymore.

Sasha nods her head but says nothing.

"Remember that time your father pitched a tent in the backyard, and we stayed up all night eating Girl Guides cookies and reading magazines together?" I ask, giggling at the memory. "It's been a long time, Sasha."

"Time?" Sasha mutters, her voice slurred. With her frail and emaciated fingers, she grasps for the rubber ball,

The Creeping Charlies

bringing it close to her chest with her head bent down over it the minute she's held on. At first, I think she might be laughing, but when I see her shoulders heaving and I hear her muffled sobs, I realize she's crying.

"Don't cry," I blurt out, falling to my knees and pulling her into a hug, my own eyes stinging with tears. "Poor Sasha. Don't cry." I can't think of anything better to say.

She grins, lifting her head for just a moment. "Poor Sasha, eh?" she says, and her eyes are savage with some eerie blaze of feral passion that burns like a wildfire.

"We'll find the time to do something fun together again," I tell her. "I promise."

"Time..." Sasha murmurs again, her eyes doe-like and big with confusion.

"Time always passes," I ramble on like an idiot, my efforts useless, "and this thing, whatever it is, it won't last forever."

"Time..." Sasha sighs, "*is* forever."

"Yes, but things change, and people change, and..."

"I wonder," says Sasha suddenly, raising her head just a little bit more to stare over my shoulder, "if the Villeneuves still have their sheepdog."

"They keep it in the basement now," I reply, "in some playroom they built for it... *why*, Sasha?"

Sasha doesn't answer me.

I don't know how she can speak anyway, when there are a million little bugs and spiders squiggling in and out of her mouth, their tiny legs brushing over her peeling lips.

"...Should we keep bouncing the rubber ball?" I ask.

The Creeping Charlies

Sasha slowly nods her head, her neck creaking stiffly, and she rises to her feet, letting the ball fall loosely from her hands with a hollow thud.

✠✠✠

It's the emptiness that gets to me the most, really.

So many rules! So much fear! Lonely days spent at the dilapidated playground I'm too old to be at, exploring the dry turquoise husks of empty swimming pools, and school is just as lonely, too. Pierre long-since dropped out of his classes. I get the little yellow bus that comes by on weekdays at the end of my street, and I ride into the next town for school. I get dirty looks from the other students. They won't sit at the desks next to mine, and they all know I'm from Charogne Falls, because the government requires that I wear a cloth face mask whenever I leave the town. It's stupid. I mean, whatever's gripping this place, it's not contagious. If my family and I could just move out, we'd be free.

Is this what's going to pass as living?

It's a cold, brittle afternoon, and I'm flipping through the TV channels, the remote control heavy in my hand while I wait for Pierre to come home from work. In the colder and shorter days of the year, it's much easier to just... withdraw from Charogne Falls altogether. I don't want to go out and see my neighbours grappling and tearing at each other while they squeeze and pull at an animal carcass, arguing over whose turn it is to take this one home. I don't want to see Mr. Themblay, the elderly crossing guard, picking through the undersides of rain gutters and laundry room vents, checking mousetraps to see if there's anything pinned down that he

The Creeping Charlies

can nibble on. I don't want to see the people who were once my friends becoming these... these mutants, these ghouls, these *things*. All they do is cry and scream, and by day, they sigh and dream. They'll be this way until they decay, until their bodies rot away...

And I'll have known them once as decent people. *That*, I think, will haunt me the most whenever we finally pack up and get out of Charogne Falls.

What will Sasha think when she discovers the house vacant? When she fails to see our vehicle in the driveway?

Will she even think anything at all?

These questions pester me like a buzzing housefly... and what better way to swat it down than with Pierre's return home? It's Saturday afternoon, and Pierre's only day off is Sunday, when he switches off his weekly holiday with Robert's. Robert's holiday is on Saturday. Maybe, I hope, Pierre will take me fishing down by the Falls, downstream where the river runs fresh, far away from the factory and far away from our street. There, the air smells as crisp as a fresh slice of watermelon on the Fourth of July, and the water sparkles and dazzles like a gemstone necklace. You could spend a day there at the riverbank, eating peanut-butter-and-lettuce sandwiches with cans of Big 8 cola, and completely forget that a few blocks away is the cautionary tale that Pierre and I call home.

"Don't leave a smear," says Mamma when she catches me with my face plastered up against the window glass. "This house is dark enough as it is without the light getting blocked off by condensation."

The Creeping Charlies

"There's already frost on it, anyway."

"Then why on earth are you trying to look out of it, Collette?"

"Because I wiped some of the frost off with my sleeve, you know, so I could watch for Pierre."

"Alright, then."

"Alright, Mamma."

Mamma gazes at me, wringing her hands the way she does when something's gone bad, the glimpse of her reflection against the window distracting me from outside. When I turn back to look at her, her eyes are shining with tears. "What's wrong, Mamma?"

"Collette... this isn't what your father and I *ever* wanted for you, for you or for Pierre, never."

"I know, Mamma. *Nobody* wanted this."

"No, you don't understand." Mamma's voice is deep and wavering, and she sits down on the sofa, burying her head in her hands. "We agreed, just about a year before you were born, to let the factory develop things for the military... things for war, things that would hurt people. We *all* agreed, the whole town. Mayor Black had it notarized, but Collette... we never thought about it."

I can barely find my own voice. My mouth feels as dry as cotton all of a sudden, and when I finally speak, I almost choke. "You never thought about *what*?"

Mamma's eyes, exhausted and bloodshot, are boring straight into the blank parlour wall where she stares. "We never thought about what it would do to other people, not until it did this to *us*."

The Creeping Charlies

What could I say? What difference would it make to protest the whole thing now?

I shiver, pressing my face back up to the window. "Pierre will be home soon, Mamma."

"I know."

"And someday, we'll all move away from Charogne Falls... right, Mamma?"

Mamma's face is blanched and pale, her upper lip twitching just the slightest bit for a moment. "We'll never be treated as a normal family if we leave Charogne Falls," she says, "and that's a lot harder to live with on a permanent basis than you might realize, Collette. It's even more difficult when you bring someone along who's..."

"Who's what?"

Mamma smiles at me, a forced smile... a scary smile. "You'll appreciate what we're doing when you're older, Collette. You want to go to university, don't you? Live in your own house, go to work, raise a family, right?"

"Sure," I reply, "I think so. Whatever."

"...Then you *will*, Collette. We just need to make some changes first."

When she leaves the room, I look up and gasp sharply, realizing that Papa's been standing in the doorway the whole time, running his hand through his brown beard as he lingers there. "Collette," he greets, nodding at me.

"Hi, Papa."

"Hi, Collette."

I can hear both of their voices, harshly whispered voices, arguing in the kitchen.

The Creeping Charlies

"You shouldn't have said anything to her yet, Dierdre. She'll only be confused now!"

"Well, she's not a little girl anymore, and I don't want her spending the rest of her childhood thinking we lied to her."

"It's not a lie! It's a... decision, a decision we both agreed on! You *saw* it last evening during supper, Dierdre. It's getting worse. The sooner we let go, the sooner we can protect our family."

"Jacque, it *scares* me!"

"It scares *me* too, Dierdre."

✠✠✠

I leap up from the sofa the minute I hear the front door creaking open, rushing forward, waiting for Pierre's usual friendly greeting.

Instead, I see Pierre leaning against the doorframe, muttering something to himself, something that doesn't make any sense at all because I can barely hear a word of it. "Long day, Pierre?" I ask with a snort of laughter, all in good fun, the same as usual.

Pierre glares at me. "Don't make jokes, Collette."

Taken aback, my mouth falls open, and I stand there in silence, completely speechless.

"What's for supper?" he barks, startling me.

"Oh, well... a leg of lamb, I think," I stammer.

"Lamb," says Pierre, in this long, bizarre, drawn-out way. "Laaammmbbb... how's it cooked?"

"I don't know," I reply with a casual shrug. "With rosemary and mint sauce, I think..."

𝒯𝒽𝑒 𝒞𝓇𝑒𝑒𝓅𝒾𝓃𝑔 𝒞𝒽𝒶𝓇𝓁𝒾𝑒𝓈

"No!" Pierre snaps. "I mean, how *much* has the meat been cooked?"

I'm more annoyed than shocked now. "Who the hell cares, Pierre? If it's too underdone, just put it in the microwave for a few minutes or something, but don't blame *me* for it!"

To my surprise, Pierre doesn't let out another rude remark my way. Instead, his lips curl up with an odd grin, and he sniffs the air vigorously. "Underdone?" he asks me.

"What's wrong with you, Pierre? Are you alright?"

Pierre pauses for a minute, eyeing me curiously... until those same eyes cloud up with guilt, and he sweeps me up in a quick embrace, just like he always does after we've bickered for a bit. "I'm sorry I startled you, Collie. It's just been a really bad day... long, cold... hazy."

"Hazy?" I whimper, the word barely loud enough for anyone but me to hear.

"Some jerk came by and threw a big rock through one of those glass brick windows on the factory," Pierre explains, rolling his eyes. "Stupid vandals, rednecks from that farming town down south... I could just rip their *heads* off if I could catch one of them."

"Gross!" I blurt out, horrified.

"I'm joking, Collie."

"I hope so!"

"Would I lie to you?" asks Pierre slowly. "To my own kid sister?"

He won't look me in the eye when he says it, and so now, I'm really not too sure.

The Creeping Charlies

✠✠✠

We're nothing like those sick people who live in the shadows of Charogne Falls.

We're *not*!

Alright, alright, so Pierre is sitting here at the table, gnawing greedily on a piece of rare lamb that's barely even touched the pot for more than five minutes, but he was working all day. Never even got a lunch break, he informed Mamma and Papa, and so he's got an excuse for the blood and juices dribbling messily down his chin while he eats.

Mamma and Papa exchange glances.

"Thank you for cooking supper, Mamma," I say, trying to break the silence, but it barely even chips the atmosphere in the room at all.

"Pierre," Papa scolds, making a face, but still unable to look away from the grisly sight before him. "Pierre, that's disgusting."

"Good lamb," Pierre grunts between mouthfuls, tearing at a fibrous hollow tube of what looks like an artery in the meat with his teeth.

"Oh god," moans Mamma, and before I know it, she's gone to the kitchen sink, vomiting straight into the steel basin that she usually makes such a strong effort to keep as spotless as when it was new.

I have no idea what to say to anyone. "Papa," I begin, stuttering, "I..."

"Don't worry, Collette," Papa sighs, giving me a sympathetic gaze across the table. "Pierre, stop that. You're scaring your sister. You know better than to eat like this."

The Creeping Charlies

Pierre ignores Papa's words, choosing instead to wipe his mouth sloppily on the back of his own hand, rising to his feet and pulling cupboards and doors open, sniffing the room. *He's hunting*, I think, and then I realize just how severe that thought of mine truly is.

"No more?" Pierre complains as he roots around through the refrigerator, shoving aside the fresh garden salad Mamma made and her delicate pink strawberry cheesecake, removing a plastic bowl covered in aluminum foil instead.

Mamma whirls around in horror at the sound of the foil rustling, her jaw dropping. "Pierre, no!" she cries, waving her hands in a frantic panic, trying to pull the bowl out of his grip. "That's not for supper! That's to go in the garbage tomorrow morning, it's..."

I can't believe my eyes when Pierre rips the bowl back out of Mamma's hands and begins digging through it, up to his arms in reeking blood, his eyes blazing wild, his teeth gnashing hungrily.

I bolt from the table and hurry as fast as I can out of the room, dizzy with nausea as I run. I can't stand it anymore. I try to make it to the staircase so I can retreat to my bedroom, but I slip on the hallway carpet and fall flat on my face, the rough fabric burning the skin of my hands raw as I struggle to find my balance.

Pierre is eating chitlins, the chitlins that Mamma had removed from a whole pig she'd bought at the butcher shop over in the next town last week, the parts we normally put in the garbage. She keeps them in the refrigerator until trash pickup day, so the neighbours won't rip open our plastic bags and strew garbage all over the front lawn as they feed on whatever they find.

Now Pierre is hunched over in the kitchen like a racoon, pulling the slippery parts from the bowl and taking bite after bite, like a starving man.

I can hear Mamma sobbing, and amidst this, Papa's useless words of reassurance. "Don't worry, Dierdre," he says, repeating it over and over as if it's some magic spell that will break us all out of this mess.

We all know better.

Pierre is sick. *Really* sick.

✠✠✠

The nighttime ritual begins as usual, but as I help Mamma to drag the oak wardrobe up against my bedroom window, we can both hear Pierre shouting and hollering as he storms from room to room, tearing the curtains straight off the walls and pulling at the nailed plywood until his fingers bleed. "Let it in!" he wails in a shrill shriek, which escalates to a mad roar the more frustrated he becomes. "There's no reason to hide, don't you all understand? No reason! It's *wonderful*! Nothing but rage, *beautiful rage!*"

"Can't you make him stop, Mamma?" I beg. "He's going to tear the *whole house* apart!"

Mamma doesn't say a word.

"He doesn't sound anything like himself anymore," I argue, my voice rendered meaningless beneath the sound of cloth being torn to shreds. Pierre is pulling down the curtains in our parents' bedroom.

The Creeping Charlies

Papa is wandering through the house, his face void of expression, like a ghost. I hear him hammering in nails again, repairing the placement of the wooden boards that Pierre ripped free from the drywall, and Mamma is curled up on my bed, weeping in a way I've never seen her weep before. Loud, hoarse sobbing that scratches at her throat like sandpaper, and she doesn't seem to care. I don't blame her.

Pierre is stomping through his own bedroom now, smashing everything that once meant something special to him. I hear the painful snapping and cracking of plastic and the tearing of thin material as my brother destroys his cassette tape collection, all the musical bands he adores, stepped on and clawed apart and thrown up against the walls like garbage, and then, as I make my way closer to his doorway, I realize that Pierre is ripping apart the stuffed teddy bear that I won for him at the carnival five years ago, the big fluffy blue bear that had once hung like a brilliant, bold trophy on a prize rack during a game of darts. I'll never forget the vexed look on the carny's paunchy face when I popped every balloon in the ring!

"Don't you want to keep your prize, Collie?" Pierre had asked, but I'd insisted. He was my older brother. He'd shown me how to play all the carnival games, how to beat the rigged ones, how to make the most of my coloured paper tickets...

And now he's popping the seams and stitches on the bear's plush body, cramming handfuls of the starchy white stuffing into his mouth, only to spit it back out and grimace. "No point," he mutters, and then, with a horrible roar that

The Creeping Charlies

leaves me shaking like a leaf in the wind, he bellows, "No point! NO POINT! It all means *nothing*!"

"Stop it!" I shout, appalled.

Pierre turns to look at me, his eyes watery and seeping a viscous yellow fluid from beneath the sockets.

"You're ruining everything!" I scream, reduced to tears. I press my eyes down into the cuffs of my blue denim jacket, dampening the fabric, and I lean against the wall, waiting for everything to be over.

Without a word to anyone, Pierre pushes his way past me and thrusts himself down the stairs, his nasty guttural moans echoing through the house as he opens the front door, fleeing into the street.

Papa slowly inches his way down the staircase soon after, huffing breathlessly, and he bolts the door shut. I can't believe it.

"…Go to bed, Collette," he tells me, and I have to force myself stiffly to make my way to the room.

✠✠✠

As usual, all through the night come the sounds of the townsfolk of Charogne Falls in the twisted throes of madness, grasping small birds and rodents, squeezing them to death, and licking the blood from their porous green hands.

Some of them, like Sasha, hunt together in packs. They creep from place to place and squabble over whatever things they can catch, and I can barely keep myself together when I hear the pained squeals of a wild rabbit being torn from one paw to the next, shaken violently by its long ears as Jerome, a

The Creeping Charlies

boy who used to be in my Grade 5 math class, crushes the animal's head.

I can see it all out my bedroom window. I've wedged my way in between the wardrobe and the window seat, wiping the crystal frost away in the hopes of being able to spot Pierre. Pierre is my brother. He's not a monster. He's always loved animals, even volunteered at the local shelter before the accident happened, and so the idea of him out there running through the darkness to hunt for live prey seems ridiculous to me.

They'll be out there until the sunrise, and then they retreat into the shadows, back into the last remnants of the lives they led before, sometimes bleaching the bloodstains from their clothes and then forgetting to hang the laundry out to dry, or washing their grimy hands with soap and hot water, only for their skin to slide right off the bones. Many of them just spend their days watching TV, because the pages of books and magazines stick like caramel taffy to their bloated fingertips. They stare at the moving pictures on the screen in this eerie, unfocused manner, their hands jittering while they drool down their chins, waiting for the night to unfold so they can go out hunting again.

No, Pierre is *nothing* like that. He always used to tell me, "Collie, if I ever get sick like they do, kill me in my sleep or something."

"*They* never *sleep, Pierre.* They stay awake all day and night."

"All the same, little sister... I won't be one of them."

The Creeping Charlies

I see Marianne LeBlanc, the girl who won the last beauty pageant in town before the accident. Her glitz dress used to be this stunning, pretty pink thing with a frilly tutu and glittering rhinestones embroidered all over it. Now Marianne's dress is soaked in mud and blood and bits of rotting animal skin. Caught on the tip of her silver tiara is a strip of raw venison that keeps flapping in the wind. I feel ill just looking at it.

Pierre would have *hated* it, being one of them.

And me? I'm a dead girl walking if we keep on staying in Charogne Falls.

✠✠✠

When I wake up the next morning, I realize that I'm not asleep in bed. I'm lying on the bare floor... and all my belongings are missing.

"Mamma!" I wail. "Papa!"

Mamma comes rushing into the room, wearing her thick wool autumn coat. She *never* wears that anymore, not since her friends have been succumbing to the accident. No need to dress to impress when you never go out for visits.

"Where's my favourite quilt?" I exclaim, trying to control my horror, but I simply can't. "Where's my oak wardrobe? Where's all my stuff?"

Mamma doesn't answer. "Come here, Collette," she says instead, wrapping her arm gently around my shoulders and leading me up to the window.

There's a rented trailer hitched to the back of our car, the door open and loaded with objects. My beloved wardrobe and quilt, all my books and clothes, my old childhood toys,

The Creeping Charlies

Mamma's pots and pans, her dressing table and silver mirror, Dad's woodworking tools and artist's canvases, our framed family photos, the sofa...

"You moved the book," is the one strange thing I can immediately think of to say.

"The book?" asks Mamma.

"Your copy of *The Bell Jar*, that one you were reading for your book club," I answer. "What did you do with it?"

"It's packed up with our other books and the wooden bookshelf from the parlour, I expect."

"Oh. Alright."

Mamma looks at me, and it's one of those stern looks of hers that I've gotten used to, but much more severe than ever before. "Your father's just rolling up the carpets from the hallways," she tells me, "and I'm going to load the television into the trunk of the car... and then *you*, Collette, I want you to get in the backseat and lock all the doors and windows. Papa will give you the keys."

"Mamma?"

"Don't ask questions, and don't unlock the car for anyone except Papa and me, do you understand? I know this is far too much for us to ask of you, but it needs to be done. If you see Sasha or Jerome or anybody else, even if you see your brother, don't roll down the window or pull the door open. Keep your head down and pretend you're not there."

"Mamma, you're scaring me..."

"I love you, Collette," Mamma interrupts, and she throws her arms around me and kisses my forehead. For a flash of a second, she's the Mamma she was when I was a little

The Creeping Charlies

girl, the cheerful, happy Mamma who loved baking cookies and playing baseball with me and Pierre in the field downtown, the Mamma who stayed up with me when I had nightmares.

It's her, and I want her back. "I love you, too," I say, clinging to her desperately. "Don't go, Mamma."

"I have to help your father," she tells me, "but don't worry, Collette. We're not going *anywhere*. We're not leaving you. When everything's ready, we're going to meet you in the car."

"And *then* what?"

"You'll see. Try to be patient."

I can be as patient as Mamma and Papa want, but I can't stand being left in the dark about things. I hurry down the staircase, throwing on my ratty old platform shoes and my pullover sweater, and then I bump into Papa in the entryway.

He doesn't say a word to me. He just nods his head and jams the car keys into my hands, and as he finishes rolling up the carpet to take outside, I run.

Pierre is there on the front porch, swinging back and forth as he grips onto one of the white columns there. "Hey, Collie," he whispers, and then he breaks into a hideous fit of giggles. "Why so melancholy, Collie?"

"What does 'melancholy' mean?" I ask him... but then I remember Mamma's words, and before I know it, I'm darting towards the car, my hands fumbling with the keys as they jangle in the breeze.

The Creeping Charlies

"Come back here!" Pierre growls, and it's then that I realize he's chasing me.

"No!" I shout at him, and when I'm finally able to get the passenger door open, I make my way inside and slam the door... right onto Pierre's spongy graying fingers, jamming them up against the metal, squishing them until they bleed... and the blood, to my shock, is all thin and congealed like fermented cod liver oil. Smells just about the same, too. Or maybe that's just Pierre's rancid breath as he roars in agony, yanking his hand back, finally allowing me to get the door closed and locked.

I try my best not to make eye contact with him. While it's been observed numerous times that they don't kill other people, the people who get sick here in Charogne Falls are unpredictable. Pierre is banging his fists over and over again on the window above me, smearing greasy blood and dirt from under his fingernails all over the glass. It's disgusting. I want to vomit, but I'm too paralyzed with dread to dare risk letting the opposite door open a crack.

When I finally lift my head, taking one single glance out the front windshield, I see two older boys and one man, wearing grayish-looking protective coats that used to be white, lead-lined hoods covering their heads and thick black gloves on their hands. All I can see are their eyes, bulging and gray with cataracts, oozing reddish fluid beneath the clear rectangles of plexiglass that make up the windows of their world. Their gloves drip with blood. One of the boys has some kind of thick beige length of entrails from an animal they've killed somewhere, and it's slung up over his shoulder, as if it's as commonplace as carrying a garden hose.

They're beckoning to Pierre, but their erratic, shaky gestures are foreign to me. I duck my head back down, shut my eyes, cover my ears and shout out songs to myself, any songs I can think of, from Christmas carols to old movie theme songs. I can't see Pierre, I can't hear him, but I can still sense that he's there.

I should have known. How could I have been so stupid?

I'd picked up the signs in Sasha's behaviour quicker than I had expected at the time, watching as she regressed further and further into this rotting husk of a life. Why hadn't I seen it in Pierre?

I guess I wanted to be optimistic. I guess I wanted to pretend that our daily existence in Charogne Falls was just the new normal we would have to live with, and it was easier than facing the truth.

It makes sense to me now, the accident, sort of. Something like this can destroy a whole town, clearly... or maybe a city, or even a *country*, if it was strong enough and plentiful enough to spread. It was an accident, so it was small, small enough to be gradually dampened down by liquidators and safety services until several years from now, it would be a neutralized threat that couldn't hurt any one of us anymore.

There would be casualties, though. We've always known that, because we were told as much, and we didn't want to believe it.

The Creeping Charlies

The rapid, pulsating blasts of a hunting rifle jolt me from my thoughts, and I shoot up in my seat, screaming.

Those horrible delusional people! When they can't catch an animal with their bare hands, they'll stalk it down and shoot it until the noise deafens them, and then they'll go out and do it again tomorrow. I *hate* it, all of it.

Pierre is nowhere to be seen, and neither are any of the other townsfolk of Charogne Falls, except for Mamma and Papa, who wave at me and beckon at the doors. When I unlock the car for them, they both reach back to my seat and hug me, as if they're never going to let me go.

"What's going on?" I demand, crossing my arms. "I'm old enough to know. You have to tell me."

"Dierdre, Collette, put your seatbelts on," says Papa, his voice unwavering, monotonous and empty. I obey, despite my anger, and I watch as Papa begins pulling out of the driveway.

I can see Sasha crawling out from under our front porch, tearing her way through a wooden beam that she's broken, dragging with her my old rubber ball. *Keep it, Sasha,* I think to myself in silence, when it finally dawns on me what's happening.

"Be careful, Jacque," says Mamma, pointing. "That dog skeleton there in the road could put a hole in our tires."

Papa nods, swerving just the slightest bit to avoid it.

"We're finally doing it," I mutter under my breath.

Mamma nods her head. "Finally."

"Where are we going to stay until we can buy a house of our own, then?"

The Creeping Charlies

Mamma smiles. "We have enough money now to drive to your Grandma Rhoda's house in Stratford. She's got two rooms set up and ready for us. We've been planning this over the telephone for a long time, Collette. It's all set up, and you'll have your own bedroom and school and lots of other people your age, people who won't know who we are or where our family came from."

I want to jump for joy, to cheer like I've never cheered before, but I can't. There's this wave of uncertainty washing over me, soaking into me, and I almost want to cry... but I don't.

"I want you to know, Collette," Mamma adds, "that we can never go back. The people here who've gotten sick, they're beyond help. They'll be the way they are until they die."

I frown, biting my lip in concern. "That's sad. You never know, Mamma. Maybe they'll be able to find a cure someday."

"It's a mutation," says Papa, "not a disease."

I try to watch out the window, to see all the things we'll be leaving behind, but all I can see through the barren strips of houses and dead forests are glimpses of people here and there, people glaring, people angry, angry at us... at *me*, for leaving. In their pallid, watery eyes and sagging faces are expressions of little else but pain.

"Keep your head down until we get past the town limits," Mamma advises. "It's easier if we don't look back, Collette."

I only wish that were true. "I left my writing notebook behind on the window seat, Mamma."

"We'll buy you another one."

"It had all my stories in it, though."

"You can write *new* stories."

New stories?

Who would ever want to read writing by somebody like me, Collette Charlie, a girl from a broken old town like Charogne Falls? And what would I possibly write about?

Maybe the bright green trees and brisk blue skies that I haven't seen in person in years. Maybe the vibrant yellow sun, or the chirping of birds, even something as simple as the whooping bark of a neighbourhood dog, a noise I used to find so annoying, but that now I can't stop yearning to hear. There are so many things I've missed that I never even thought to miss before. When was the last time I felt the soft fluffy petals of a golden dandelion flower under my fingertips? When was the last time I inhaled the fresh summery scent of newly-mown grass? When was the last time I splashed in a rain puddle without worrying about what was in the water, or jumped up and down on the trampoline in my backyard, reaching out to try and touch the clouds?

I sink back against my seat, staring straight ahead, avoiding the side windows altogether. "What about Pierre? Will he be alright in Charogne Falls with all the rest of them?"

Papa gazed at me through the rear-view mirror. There were tears glistening in his eyes, but still he kept driving. "I shot Pierre, Collette. Pierre is dead."

The Creeping Charlies

Mamma holds back a sob, but then utters, "just keep driving, Jacque. Please."

They both make it sound so easy... to just keep on going, going on without looking back.

Goodbye, Charogne Falls.

✠✠✠

If one day I happen to be in another place of mystery, maybe I'll know better, from my experience, how to cope.

For now, I don't ever want to think of Charogne Falls again.

We've arrived now in Berwick, a small community in Ontario, parking at a Petro-Canada station so Papa can refill the car. The sky is gray... not a sickly white, but a clean, safe, fresh rainy gray that makes me feel alive every time I breathe it in. The warm green grass is alluring and bright against my pale skin when I bend down to touch it. It's soft, not crispy and yellow the way the grass in Charogne Falls is.

Mamma and Papa have sent me into the convenience store to buy some food and drinks for us all to share. We might've gone through a drive-thru, but fast food is a bit beyond our budget right now. Until one of us gets a job, money's going to be tight for a while.

The sensory feelings almost cause me to faint right there on the floor of the store, my knees weak as I walk through the sea of colourful rainbow aisles, of numerous foil bags of potato chips and cold cans of pop and iced tea, of assorted gummy animals and chocolate bars...

And when I hear the soft sounds of mewling nearby, at first I think I must be having some sort of bizarre dream.

The Creeping Charlies

"What's that noise?" I ask the cashier as he adds up all my items at the register.

The cashier points down behind the counter at his feet, and when I lean over it to see what's down there, I'm greeted by a cardboard box with a kitten in it, nestled in a soft blue terrycloth towel and peering up at me with the most beautiful emerald eyes, eyes untainted by the world.

"Dolores, my cat, she had kittens awhile back," the cashier explained sheepishly, running a hand through his shaggy red hair. "Found homes for three of them, but this fourth one here..."

I don't know what compels me, but before I realize what I'm even saying, I declare loudly, "I'll buy the kitten, Sir!"

Surprise washes over the man's freckled face. "You want the kitten? It's the runt of the litter, you know. Just a mongrel cat at that, mixed-breed..."

"Perfect," I say, and as I count out my money to pay him for it, he lifts the box in his arms and slides it over to me.

"How much are you selling it for?" I ask.

"Don't bother," says the cashier, grinning. "I just want to see Dolores's kittens going to decent people. Promise me you'll take good care of it, alright, kid?"

I agree, but the promise is by no means necessary.

Papa is standing there in the parking lot, tapping his foot on the asphalt impatiently when I return to the car, the grocery bags hanging off my elbows. "Glad you could join us again, Collette," he says, and at first I'm worried that he's angry with me... but to my relief, a huge smile emerges from his bearded face, and he laughs. "Just joking," he adds, and then I can't help laughing, either.

I haven't seen Papa smile like that in ages.

When I pull Mamma's car door open, I can see that she's been crying the whole time I've been gone. She has a disposable tissue box beside her, her face damp and puffy, and she looks completely drained. "Wrong door, Collette," she tells me, motioning to the backseat.

It's time, I think, *to turn over a new leaf.*

I slide the cardboard box onto Mamma's lap, watching her face light up when she lifts the flaps and looks inside. She gasps, and the tears I see in her eyes then are tears of joy.

"Mamma," I announce, smiling as I watch her cuddle the tiny kitten into the crook of her neck, stroking its fleecy fur, "I want you to meet…"

What should the kitten's name be?

I observe the kitten's fur, not quite white but not beige, either. It's a kind of creamy buttermilk colour.

"Mamma… this is Parsnip. Parsnip Charlie."

We're going to be alright, aren't we?

About the Author

Rebecca Maye Holiday is a Nova Scotian author, her most popular book being *Necromancy Cottage, Or, The Black Art of Gnawing on Bones*. She also writes literary short stories and smaller novellas. She studies law and the occult through a dual degree at Dalhousie University and The University of King's College in Halifax, and she has a diploma in library information technology from the Nova Scotia Community College, awarded in 2018.

Milton Keynes UK
Ingram Content Group UK Ltd.
UKHW010158190124
436283UK00001B/2